WALLY'S DETECTIVE BOOK FOR SOLVING PROBLEMS AT HOME

Written by Carolyn Webster-Stratton, Ph.D.

Wally's directions for parents and teachers about how to use this book

Make reading this book a fun game.
Wally's detective book will become more useful with time and repetition. This book is best read to children by teachers and parents in short intervals, perhaps doing three or four of the problems in one reading. Make the problem-solving game fun, and praise the children's ideas for solutions with phrases such as, "Wow! You are a great detective. You're thinking of so many ideas." You and your child might even keep score of how many solutions you come up with on Wally's solution score card. However, the main idea is not to force children to come up with "right" answers to the problems (or the same ones as Wally) but rather to help them think about the conflict situations and generate as many ideas as they can. It is the generation of ideas that is important.

Act out solutions.
Children also like to role play or act out their solutions. They find it fun if you ask them to show you how they would actually solve the problem. The parent, teacher or another child can play the part of the child with the problem, and several other children can act out their solutions. This acting is not only fun but it helps children better understand the possible consequences of their solutions.

For young preschool children, focus on generating solutions.
For very young children to start, you may need to suggest or model some possible ideas for solutions. You may even ask the children to draw their own ideas for solutions so that they can make their own detective solution book.

For older children (ages 5 to 8 years).
As children become comfortable generating solutions you can ask them some of the following questions to help them learn to evaluate their solutions.

• Do you think the solution is fair?
• Does the solution lead to good feelings? How would you feel if someone did that?
• Is the solution safe?
• What do you think would happen next if you tried the solution? This helps the child think ahead and anticipate the consequences.
• Is there another solution that might work?
• Which solution do you think is the best one to try first?
• If the solution didn't work, what would you do next? Prepare children for the possibility their solution may not work.

Explore feelings.
Each of the problem situations presented here evokes different kinds of feelings such as disappointment, sadness, fear, anxiety, embarrassment, frustration, and anger. As you read and discuss the problem with children ask them how the characters in the story are feeling and help the children put labels to the feelings i.e., to name their feelings. Labeling feelings is key to children learning better regulation of their emotional responses. Only when children can put a word to a feeling and express it to someone else can they begin to feel some self- control over the situation.

Make it personal.
As you discuss the hypothetical problem situations and explore the feelings and possible solutions, you can ask children about their own experiences with similar problems.

• Have you ever had a problem like that or felt that way about something?
• How did you solve it?

Wally's instructions to detectives in training

Let's see how good your detective skills are! In this book Wally Problem-Solver presents you with a problem to solve. Think of a possible solution or even more than one solution if you can! Then turn to the corresponding pages in the back of the book containing Wally's solutions, and see if you had any of the same ideas that Wally had. Give yourself a point for every solution of yours that is the same as Wally's. Give yourself a bonus point if you had a different solution. See if you can earn enough points to get in Wally's detective club.

Remember when you think of a solution to ask yourself:
Is it fair?
Does it lead to good feelings?
Is it safe?

LEVEL 1. POINTS
1 2 3 4 5
6 7 8 9 10
11 12 13 14 15

CONGRATULATIONS. YOU ARE IN WALLY'S DETECTIVE CLUB!

LEVEL 2. POINTS
16 17 18 19 20
21 22 23 24 25

WOW! SUPER DETECTIVE!

LEVEL 3. POINTS
26 27 28 29 30 31
32 33 34 35

MEGA POWER!

Problem-Solving Case 1:
"I want it! You can't have it!"

Molly and Wally both want to watch a different program on television and they get into a fight. What should they do?

Think about your own solutions and then turn to page 27 to see if you found any of Wally's ideas.

Problem-Solving Case 2:
"My cat died."

Felicity's cat has died and she is crying. What should she do?

Think about your own solutions first and then turn to page 28 to see if you found any of Wally's ideas.

Problem-Solving Case 3:
"It's all my fault."

When Oscar the Ostrich's parents argue he hides his head in the sand - afraid. He thinks they are fighting because of him. What should he do?

Think about your own solutions and then turn to page 29 to see if you found any of Wally's ideas.

Problem-Solving Case 4: "I lied."

Felicity has broken her mother's vase but she is scared to tell her. Instead she tells a lie blaming her brother. What should she do?

Think about your own solutions and then turn to page 30 to see if you found any of Wally's ideas.

Problem-Solving Case 5:
"I won't."

Molly's mom asks her to set the table just as her favorite TV program is about to start. What should she do?

Think about your own solutions and then turn to page 31 to see if you found any of Wally's ideas.

Problem-Solving Case 6: "He won't help me."

Big Red's friend won't help him clean up the toys in his family's living room even though his mother has asked them to. What should he do?

Think about your own solutions first and then turn to page 32 to see if you found any of Wally's ideas.

Problem-Solving Case 7: "I blew it."

Wally's dad says he won't take him to the baseball game because Wally fought with his sister. What should he do?

Think about your own solutions first and then turn to page 32 to see if you found any of Wally's ideas.

Problem-Solving Case 8:
"He won't do anything."

Freddy has a friend over and his friend doesn't want to do anything he suggests doing. What should he do?

Think about your own solutions first and then turn to page 33 to see if you found any of Wally's ideas.

Problem-Solving Case 9:
"What's wrong?"

Felicity is afraid because she has seen her mom crying. What should she do?

Think about your own solutions first and then turn to page 33 to see if you found any of Wally's ideas.

Problem-Solving Case 10: "It's mine, no it's mine."

Molly and Wally are both going to different camps and there is only one camera which they both want to use. What should they do?

Think about your own solutions first and then turn to page 34 to see if you found any of Wally's ideas.

Problem-Solving Case 11:
"I'm scared."

Big Red has been invited to stay overnight at Freddy's house. He has never stayed overnight at a friend's house before. He feels anxious about leaving home and sleeping in someone else's room. He hasn't told his friend but he is scared of the dark and sleeps with his light on. He is thinking he shouldn't go because he won't be able to sleep. How do you think he can solve his problem?

Think about your own solutions first and then turn to page 35 to see if you found any of the same solutions as Wally?

Problem-Solving Case 12: "My dad's angry."

Oscar's dad seems angry and says he's had a bad day. What can Oscar do?

Think about your own solutions first and then turn to page 35 to see if you found any of Wally's ideas.

Problem-Solving Case 13: "I lost it."

Tiny lost his jacket at school for the second time. What should he do?

Think about your own solutions first and then turn to page 36 to see if you found any of Wally's ideas.

Problem-Solving Case 14:
"My friends want me to do it, but should I?"

Freddy's friend wants him to bike down to the store to get some candy, but his mother has said he is not to go beyond the front yard. What should he do?

Think about your own solutions first and then turn to page 36 to see if you found any of Wally's ideas.

Problem-Solving Case 15:
"Just this time."

Felicity is only allowed to watch one hour of TV a day. Her favorite show comes on but she's already watched her hour of TV. Her mom asks her how much TV she has watched. What should she do?

Think about your own solutions first and then turn to page 37 to see if you found any of Wally's ideas.

Problem-Solving Case 16: "I can't do it."

Oscar tries riding a bicycle but he keeps falling down over and over again. He thinks to himself, "I can't do it. I can't do it." What should he do?

Think about your own solutions first and then turn to page 38 to see if you found any of Wally's ideas.

Problem-Solving Case 17:
"No one likes me."

Tiny Turtle feels lonely and left out. No one invites him to their house after school or during weekends. He never gets invited to birthday parties or to join other kids' clubs. He's afraid to invite someone over to his house because he thinks they'll refuse. What should he do?

Think about your own solutions first and then turn to page 39 to see if you found any of Wally's ideas.

Problem-Solving Case 18:
"It's not fair."

Molly's brother Wally used her paint set without asking her permission and it's all messed up. She is really angry. What should she do?

Think about your own solutions first and then turn to page 40 to see if you found any of Wally's ideas.

Problem Solving Case 19:
"I look terrible."

Felicity had her hair cut and styled and she thinks she looks stupid. She is very embarrassed.

Think about your own solutions first and then turn to page 41 to see if you found any of Wally's ideas.

Problem Solving Case 20:
"How can I join in?"

Freddy is at the playground near his house and a group of kids are playing a game. He doesn't know any of them and wants to join in and play with them but he is unsure what to do.

Think about your own solutions first and then turn to page 41 to see if you found any of Wally's ideas.

Problem Solving Case 21: "She stole my friend."

Molly is worried because her best friend Felicity has a new friend with whom she has been spending a lot of time. Molly doesn't like the new friend very much. She's afraid this new friend is going to steal Felicity from her as a friend. What should Molly do?

Think about your own solutions first and then turn to page 42 to see if you found any of Wally's ideas.

Problem Solving Case 22:
"It's not my fault."

Big Red's little brother keeps messing up their bedroom and
getting into his things. Big Red gets into trouble for not
cleaning up when it is really his brother who is making the
mess. His mother tells him he should be more responsible
because he is older.

Think about your own solutions first and then turn to page 43
to see if you found any of Wally's ideas.

Solutions

Problem 1

Solution: Take it in turns.

Solution: Flip a coin.

Problem 2

Solution: Allow yourself to cry and feel sad.

Solution: Ask for a hug.

Solution: When you're ready, you can make a new friend after you lose an old one.

Solution: Do something tha will make you feel good.

I AM FEELING SAD. IT MIGHT HELP ME FEEL BETTER IF I DO SOMETHING THAT WILL MAKE ME FEEL GOOD.

Problem 3

Solution: Tell your parents how you are feeling.

Solution: Go somewhere safe and get help if necessary.

Problem 4

Solution: Admit what you've done.

Solution: Offer to repair the damage.

Solution: Apologize.

Problem 5

Solution: Ask if you can set the table later.

Solution: Suggest doing a different chore
after your program has finished.

Solution: Quickly set the table.

Problem 6

Solution: Ask him again.

Solution: Reward yourself!

Problem 7

Solution: Apologize.

Solution: Go to a quiet place and calm down.

Problem 8

Solution: Ask your friend what he would like to do.

Solution: Suggest another idea.

Problem 9

Solution: Ask what's the matter.

Solution: Ask if you can help.

Problem 10

Solution: Flip a coin.

Solution: Negotiate.

Solution: Bargain.

Solution: Be generous.

Problem 11

Solution: Think good thoughts and stop fearful thoughts.

Solution: Make a plan.

Problem 12

Solution: Be considerate.

Solution: Say how you feel.

Problem 13

Solution: Admit what you've done.

Solution: Make a plan.

Problem 14

Solution: Say, "No I can't."

Solution: Congratulate yourself!

Problem 15

Solution: Tell the truth.

Solution: Compromise.

Problem 16

Solution: Don't give up and try again.

Solution: Get some help.

Solution: Think helpful thoughts.

Problem 17

Solution: Think courageous thoughts and keep trying.

Solution: Do something you'll enjoy.

Problem 18

Solution: Say how you feel.

Solution: Calm down first.

Problem 19

Solution: Think good thoughts.

Problem 20

Solution: Watch, wait and praise.

Solution: Wait for pause in game and then ask to join in.

Problem 21

Solution: Respect your friend's decisions.

Solution: Make other friends.

Solution: Stay loyal to your friend.

Problem 22

Solution: Explain your point of view.

Solution: Make a plan.